The Mega Monkey Mystery

Pigs CAN fly!

Kweeeeeeeeeeeeeeeeeeeeeeeeep!

When the Alarm Squeal sounds it must
be a job for Captain Peter Porker and
the PIGS IN PLANES!

Paul Cooper is from Manchester.
He now lives in Cambridge with
his wife and two daughters.

Read these high-flying adventures
about the Pigs in Planes:

The Mega Monkey Mystery

PAUL COOPER

Illustrated by Trevor Dunton

PUFFIN

PUFFIN BOOKS

Published by the Penguin Group
Penguin Books Ltd, 80 Strand, London WC2R 0RL, England
Penguin Group (USA) Inc., 375 Hudson Street, New York, New York 10014, USA
Penguin Group (Canada), 90 Eglinton Avenue East, Suite 700, Toronto, Ontario, Canada M4P 2Y3
(a division of Pearson Penguin Canada Inc.)
Penguin Ireland, 25 St Stephen's Green, Dublin 2, Ireland (a division of Penguin Books Ltd)
Penguin Group (Australia), 250 Camberwell Road, Camberwell, Victoria 3124, Australia
(a division of Pearson Australia Group Pty Ltd)
Penguin Books India Pvt Ltd, 11 Community Centre, Panchsheel Park, New Delhi – 110 017, India
Penguin Group (NZ), 67 Apollo Drive, Rosedale, North Shore 0632, New Zealand
(a division of Pearson New Zealand Ltd)
Penguin Books (South Africa) (Pty) Ltd, 24 Sturdee Avenue, Rosebank, Johannesburg 2196, South Africa

Penguin Books Ltd, Registered Offices: 80 Strand, London WC2R 0RL, England

puffinbooks.com

First published 2010
1

Text copyright © Paul Cooper, 2010
Illustrations copyright © Trevor Dunton, 2010
All rights reserved

The moral right of the author and illustrator has been asserted

Set in Bembo Infant
Made and printed in England by Clays Ltd, St Ives plc

British Library Cataloguing in Publication Data
A CIP catalogue record for this book is available from the British Library

ISBN: 978–0–141–32844–7

www.greenpenguin.co.uk

For Heidi, Chuck, Sam and Harry

MEET THE CREW

TAMMY SNUFFLES,

Mechanic

BRIAN TROTTER,

Medical Officer

CURLY McHOGLET,

Trainee

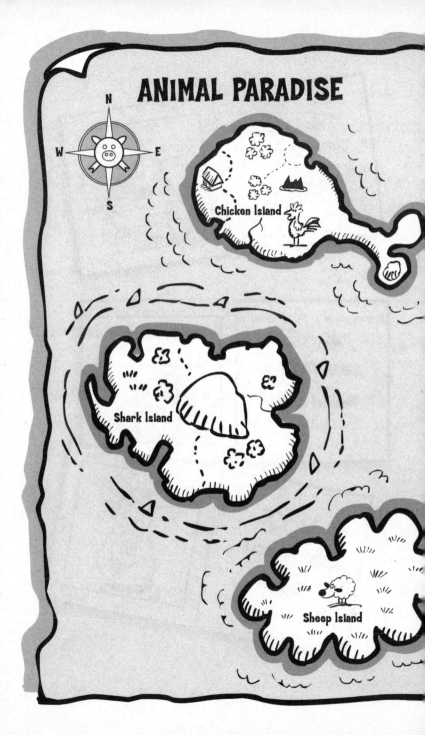

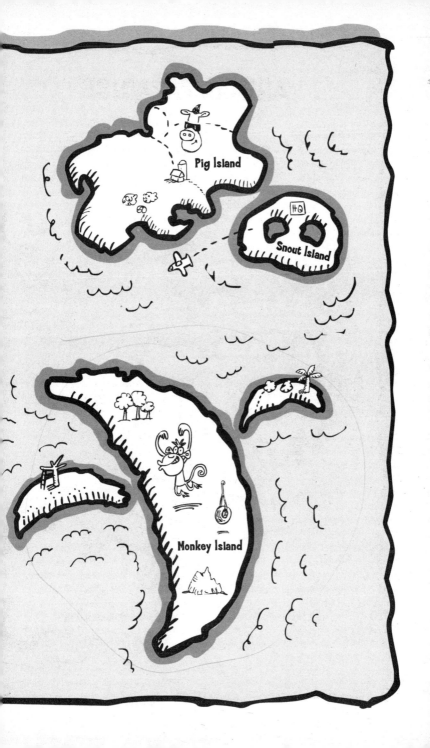

CHAPTER 1:

Smile!

The first thing Wing Commander Peregrine Oinks-Gruntington saw when he came into the Pigs in Planes common room was a huge, horrible face with great big eyes like two poached eggs staring right at him.

'AAARGH!' he cried. 'Intruder in the HQ!'

'It's OK, Peregrine!' laughed Captain Peter Porker from the sofa. 'That's just Brian's latest masterpiece!'

Once his heart had stopped thudding and his moustache had relaxed to its usual shape, Peregrine saw it was true: the awful face was just a painting.

Curly McHoglet, the PiPs' latest recruit, quickly explained that Brian had decided to take up art as a hobby. The medical officer now spent all his spare time 'creating masterpieces' (his words). He'd propped this one up near the door to dry while he moved on to his next work of art.

Peregrine studied the painting. He squinted in case that might help. 'What's it meant to be?' he asked at last.

Brian was just coming back into the room behind him. He was wearing an artist's smock, with a neat little black beret on his head, and carrying a bowl of fruit in his trotters. 'It's a self-portrait,' he announced.

'Of who?' asked Curly.

'Me, obviously!' cried Brian. 'The style is influenced by Pig Island's greatest artist, Pigasso.' He saw the blank look on the young trainee's face and sighed. 'Are you familiar with Pigasso's portraits? They do look a bit weird.'

'Oh . . .' Curly was still confused. 'Um . . . why?'

Pete jumped in to help. 'Have you never seen a photo of Pigasso? He was one weird-looking pig himself.'

'Really?' asked Curly.

'Let's just say, he was no oil painting,' said Pete.

Peregrine stomped off, muttering something about what the modern generation was coming to. Brian tried to ignore all of this. He knew artists had to suffer for their art, but surely there had to be limits. Anyway, he needed to concentrate on his next work, a still-life painting of a bowl of fruit. It took him ages to arrange the fruit on the table until it was just so.

Finally he stepped back to his easel and began to slap paint on. He was aware of his team-mates watching every brushstroke.

'You're doing the apple!' cried Curly,

recognizing the swirl of red on the canvas. 'It looks like an apple, too!'

Brian nodded. 'Yes, but I'm not just painting the outside of the apple ... As an artist, I want to get INSIDE the apple.'

Curly blinked. 'Like a maggot?'

'No, no,' Brian cried. 'You see ... when I paint the apple, it's as if I AM the apple. Do you understand?'

'Oh, we understand.' Pete's grin stretched across his snout. 'But you're not an apple, Brian – you're a nut!'

The door slammed behind them and the PiPs mechanic, Tammy Snuffles, came into the common room. 'Did someone mention food? I need a snack!'

She marched up to the bowl on the table and grabbed an apple from the top. Before anyone could stop her she chomped into it, sending a spray of juice and pips everywhere.

Brian couldn't believe his eyes. 'WHAT are you doing?'

Tammy took a second bite. 'Just having one of my five a day,' she replied through a mouthful of apple.

Brian threw down his brush. 'Great! Now I'm going to have to get more fruit!' He stomped off, complaining, 'Why are artistic geniuses never understood?'

'Sorry, Bri!' Tammy called after him. She looked at the other pigs and shrugged. 'Do you think he'd mind if I had a banana as well?'

But there was no time for anyone to reply. Just as Brian returned with a fresh supply of fruit, the Alarm Squeal sounded.

'*KWEEEEEEEEEEEEEEEEEEEEEEEE EEEEEEEEEEEEEEEEEEEEEEP!*'

Somewhere in Animal Paradise there was a problem that only the Pigs in Planes could handle.

Brian immediately pulled off his beret and smock: he was no longer Brian Trotter, misunderstood artist; now he was Brian Trotter, medical officer in the world-famous crime-fighting, jet-flying Pigs in Planes!

As the PiPs ran for the exit, he glanced sideways at Tammy.

'What's that you're eating?' he asked suspiciously.

'Nothing,' Tammy answered, quickly swallowing her mouthful of banana.

Minutes later three SkyHog jets were in the air, with trainee Curly in the passenger seat of Pete's plane.

As usual, the PiPs radio operator, Lola Penn, detailed the mission over the radio. 'Set your flight course for Monkey Island,' she told them. 'You'll like this mission, Brian. You're going to an *art* gallery.'

Lola explained that their destination was the world-famous National Primate Gallery, the home of the finest works of art in all of Animal Paradise.

'Don't they keep the *Mona Fleasa* there?' asked Tammy.

The *Mona Fleasa* was the most famous painting in Animal Paradise. Painted more than four hundred years ago, it showed a young monkey with her hands calmly folded in front of her dark dress. But the most memorable thing about it was the smile on the monkey's face.

'Ooh, we learnt about the *Mona Fleasa* at school!' Curly piped up. 'I always wondered about that funny little smile on her face. What IS she smiling at anyway?'

Brian's voice came over the radio. 'The *Mona Fleasa's* smile is the most famous in art history. It's usually described as . . .'

'Weird?' cut in Tammy.

'Toothy?' guessed Pete. 'Smug? Gappy? Creepy?'

'. . . *mysterious*,' said Brian. 'No one really knows why she's smiling. It's art's greatest unanswered question – hundreds of books have been written about it.' Brian sounded

suddenly nervous as an awful idea hit him.
'Lola, please tell me nothing has happened
to the *Mona Fleasa*!'

'Nothing has happened to the *Mona
Fleasa . . .*' said Lola.

Brian let out a long breath. 'Thank
goodness!' he said.

'. . . except it isn't there,' the radio operator
finished.

Brian was so surprised he jerked the
controls and his SkyHog wobbled in mid-
air. 'What?' he cried. 'The greatest art
treasure in all of Animal Paradise has been
stolen? When?'

'Let's see. It happened –' there was a rustle
of papers as Lola checked the details – 'three
days ago.'

The SkyHogs were flying at top speed
to Monkey Island, but suddenly their speed
didn't seem to matter so much.

'Erm, they've waited a long time to

call us, haven't they?' said Tammy. 'I'm no expert on art theft, but the robbers could have stopped for a weekend city break and they'd *still* have had time to make a clean getaway!'

'I agree it's strange,' said Lola. 'You'd better get to the museum as soon as you can. The curator there is a colobus monkey called Robin Pedalbin. I'm sure he'll explain everything. Good luck, PiPs!'

CHAPTER 2:

From the Art

The SkyHogs entered the airspace of the
Banana Republic of Monkey Island and
began their descent over the capital, Simian
City. They landed in the car park in front of
the National Primate Gallery.

'Oi, you can't leave those there!' hooted a
howler monkey parking attendant.

But Pete just waved him away. 'Don't
worry! They're a new outdoor art
installation!'

The four PiPs ran between the tall
columns that guarded the grand entrance
to the biggest art gallery in all of Animal

Paradise. Once inside, Brian was thrilled.
While Pete looked for someone in charge,
the medic looked around excitedly. 'We're in
the modern art wing!' he explained.

Curly looked at the various objects in the
huge white room. In one corner there was
a giant skull made out of old soup cans. In
another there was what looked like a stack
of wood with an old bike lying across it.

'Someone's dumped a load of rubbish
over there!' the trainee PiP said.

'That's the *art!*' tutted Brian. He guided Curly towards a huge painting. 'Here, look at this piece.'

Curly looked at the explosions of colour on the canvas. 'What's it supposed to be?' he asked, puzzled.

'It's not supposed to BE anything,' explained Brian. 'What do you think the artist is trying to say?'

Curly stared some more at the splatters of red and yellow on the canvas.

Tammy came up behind them. 'I think the artist is trying to say, "Watch out! Some nutter's going to chuck a load of pizzas at the wall!"'

Brian sighed. 'To me, this is a bold exploration of the idea of personal freedom in the modern world. What's it called anyway?'

Curly went closer and read out the label. 'It's called *Who ordered all these pizzas?*'

Tammy grinned, but the medic was already moving swiftly along.

'Now here's an interesting piece,' he told the others. He was pointing to a small red box with a glass circle in the middle. 'Pay particular attention to the artist's use of shape and colour.'

'Really?' asked Curly. He went closer.

'Don't touch!' hissed Brian, and he pointed at a sign on the wall:

DO <u>NOT</u> TOUCH THE ART WITH FINGERS, FEATHERS, CLAWS, HOOVES OR TROTTERS!

'Also, you might create a disturbance,' said a cold voice from behind them. 'You are looking at the fire alarm.'

Brian noticed the words BREAK GLASS IN CASE OF EMERGENCY in red capitals on the glass circle. 'I knew that!' he spluttered, going red about the cheeks and turning round.

The owner of the cold voice was a tall colobus monkey. His long black hair was swept back dramatically, and the white bits at the sides made him look very important. He was smartly dressed and in one hand he carried a smart black case.

It was clear that he was the top banana in the museum.

'Are you Mr Pedalbin?' Curly asked brightly.

The tall monkey sniffed. 'The correct way to say my name is "Pe-DAL-bin". But yes, I am he.'

'Ah, there you are,' said

Pete, coming up behind the group. 'You must be Mr Pedalbin then?'

The monkey sniffed again. 'The *correct* way to say my name is . . .' He looked at Pete, then sighed as if to say *Why bother?* 'Yes, I am he.'

'We're the Pigs in Planes,' Pete said, reaching for his comb. (He always did this when someone's hairstyle rivalled the pride and joy on top of his own head.)

'I know perfectly well who – and what – you are,' answered Pedalbin coolly. 'There is very little time. Walk this way.'

He spun around and headed back towards the main area of the museum, the knuckles of his free hand dragging on the floor.

'I *can't* walk that way,' whispered Pete to the others. 'My arms aren't long enough!'

They followed the curator through several long galleries. Every time they walked past one of the museum's baboon security guards, Pedalbin nodded. In one room, Brian pointed excitedly at a famous monkey statue. It was very old and both of its arms had broken off long ago.

Tammy clapped a trotter over Curly's eyes. 'You're too young to see that,' she said. 'That statue's got no clothes on!'

'Yes, but he looks *armless* enough,' said Pete with a grin. 'D'ya get it?'

Pedalbin glanced back. 'Unfortunately, yes,' he said without a smile. His sense of humour seemed to be missing along with the gallery's most famous painting.

The curator led them into one last room. This was the only place in the whole building devoted to the works of a single artist – the famous Leo Nardo, a monkey genius who had lived hundreds of years ago.

Curly looked around with big eyes at all the priceless paintings. 'One monkey did all of these pictures? WOW! He was good at drawing and colouring in.'

Pedalbin arched an eyebrow. 'Leo Nardo was the greatest artistic genius who ever scampered across the earth. So, yes, he was –' he spat the words – '*really quite good at COLOURING IN!*'

'He wasn't just a painter either,' Brian added eagerly. 'He was interested in science too.' The medic pointed to a series of sketches on the wall. Some of them were detailed drawings of muscles and tendons and how they worked. Others were ideas for amazing new inventions.

'He drew loads of designs for flying-machines,' raved Brian, 'centuries before the first plane was invented! None of them ever worked, but he definitely understood the principles of flight.'

This is more like it, Tammy thought. She wasn't too interested in fine art, but she

loved a nice bit of engineering design.

Pedalbin shuddered as the PiPs mechanic leaned in closer to the sketches. 'Don't go too near them with those horrible mucky trotters!' he barked. 'In fact, all of you – just stand in the middle of the room, don't touch anything, and direct your attention over *here*.'

The PiPs followed the monkey's long finger to an empty spot on the wall. 'There's nothing there,' said Curly.

'Precisely!' said Pedalbin. 'But what *should* be there is the *Mona Fleasa*!'

'How did the thieves manage to get in and out?' asked Pete. 'You've got security, haven't you?'

'We have the best security system money can buy!' snapped Pedalbin. 'CCTV cameras, laser trip-wires, state-of-the-art motion sensors. The video footage shows nothing,' he admitted. 'One moment it's there and the next it's gone.'

Pete shrugged. 'Strange! I'd ask for your money back, if I were you.'

Ignoring this, Pedalbin went on. 'The thieves contacted us yesterday. They have offered to give the painting back, in exchange for a ransom.'

'You're not going to give those criminals what they want, are you?' piped up Curly.

Pedalbin bared his teeth in a display of irritation. 'The Primate Minister herself thinks we cannot risk losing our greatest art treasure. For this reason, we have agreed to pay.'

'How much?' asked Tammy.

In answer, Pedalbin opened the case he'd

been carrying. It was stuffed full of crisp, yellow 100-Nana bills.

Tammy let out a low whistle. 'You could buy a lot of pizzas with all that cash.'

'We want the PiPs to carry out the handover for us.' Pedalbin passed Pete a card with an address on it. 'You will take the money to this telephone box at precisely two o'clock. The thieves will call and issue further instructions. So that you can be sure it is them, they will address you by the code-name "Mr Pink". Do you have any questions?'

'Yes,' said Pete. 'Do I have to be *Mr Pink*? I'd rather be Mr Red. Or Yellow's good . . .'

Judging from the number of teeth on display, Pedalbin was getting cross. 'After you have safely returned the *Mona Fleasa*, I don't care if you call yourself *Mr All-the-Colours-of-the-Rainbow*!' he snapped. 'But until that time, you will follow my instructions to the letter.'

As Pedalbin left them to get ready, it was clear that Curly wasn't happy about the mission. 'I don't like just handing over money to rotten criminals!' the trainee complained.

'Neither do I,' agreed Brian.

'We're a top, porcine crime-fighting unit, not a delivery service!' added Tammy.

Pete looked at the case full of money. 'I agree . . . But what if there's a way of getting the painting back AND catching the criminals?' he suggested.

'That sounds more like it!' said Curly.

Pete looked over at Tammy. 'Got any nifty gadgets we could use?'

The mechanic grinned. 'I can fit you with a mini-radio,' she said. 'That way we can monitor your every move when you make the handover. Also . . .' She dug into her backpack and pulled out a small metal

object with
a dial on the
side.

'What is it?'
asked Curly.

'It's a
paint bomb,'
explained
Tammy. 'We
set the timer
and then pack it in the side flap of the case.
When the timer goes off – POOF! It will
spray paint all over the place. It won't be
hard finding the robbers if they're covered in
paint!'

'So we'll catch them red-handed?' asked
Curly eagerly.

'Sort of,' said Tammy. 'Except it's purple
paint.'

Only Brian sounded a note of caution.
'Are we *sure* about this?' he asked. 'What if

something goes wrong?'

Pete grinned. 'C'mon, Bri. What could possibly go wrong? It'll be a walk in the park.'

CHAPTER 3:

A Run in the Park

The telephone box was in a quiet part of Simian City, so there weren't many monkeys walking along the pavement or swinging from tree to tree.

As the instructions had stated, Pete went to the meeting place alone with the case. However, the instructions had said nothing about wearing a hidden mini-radio; Pete's was under the baseball cap that he'd borrowed from Tammy. The rest of the team were sitting in one of the gallery's jeeps just a block away – they'd be able to hear everything and could provide back-up at any moment.

Pete stepped into the phone box at a minute to the hour. He glanced at his watch and then . . .

BRRRING! BRRRRING!

Pete grabbed the phone.

'Mr Pink?' said a low voice.

'Sorry, no one here by that name,' Pete answered. 'This is a kebab shop, mate.'

There was a long silence on the line, and then a doubtful 'Really?'

'Nah, just kidding!' Pete grinned. He liked to try to inject a little humour into tense situations. 'I AM Mr Pink.'

'Well then, I hope you're in good shape, Mr Pink,' said the voice on the line, sounding calm again.

'Let's just say, I work out at the gym at least once – sometimes twice – a year.' Pete caught his own reflection in the phone-box window and winked.

'Good. Because you have exactly two minutes to reach the telephone box on the corner of Lemur and Swing Streets, starting . . . NOW!'

'Wait!' Pete shouted. 'I'm not sure where that is . . .' But the line had gone dead.

Pete burst out of the phone box and shouted into the radio mike, 'Did you get all that?'

'We did!' answered Tammy. 'Bri's just looking it up in the A–Z.' A couple of seconds later she began to relay directions to Pete. 'You'll have to cut through the park to your west! But we can't follow you, we'll have to drive the long way round. You're on your own, Captain!'

Pete ran as fast as he could. He liked speed, but only when it involved sitting on a motorbike or in a powerboat or – best of all – in the cockpit of SkyHog 1. Where was the fun in going fast

by RUNNING? It was too much
effort for too little speed.

His legs agreed, which is why they
were aching by the time he spotted
the next phone box on the other side
of the park. He was still twenty metres
away when the phone started to ring.

Pete put on a final sprint, and
pulled the phone off the hook.

'Almost too late, Mr Pink,' teased
the deep voice on the other end.

'GAAAAAAAH!' said Pete, mainly
because this was all his lungs allowed
him to say just now.

'No jokes?' continued the voice.

'GAH!' said Pete. It was still the best reply he could come up with, under the circumstances.

'Good. You now have another two minutes to get to the phone box on the corner of Howler and Squirrel Streets. I'll start timing as soon as you hear the . . .'

CLICK! went the phone.

Pete stumbled out of the phone box.

'Can you hear me, Pete?' came Tammy's voice over the radio.

'GAAH!'

'You need to go north and take the second left. Oh, and Pete?'

'GAH?'

'It's a long way, so run! Run like the wind!'

Pete's trotters pounded against the pavement. His legs ached, his lungs ached, his . . . *everything* ached. He felt his heartbeat pulsing in his forehead and he was pretty sure that wasn't a good sign. The suitcase full of Nana notes seemed to weigh a ton, but he couldn't abandon it.

Pete forced himself to carry on. At last, he could see the little red phone box in the distance, like a vision shimmering before the eyes of someone in the desert who really wanted to make a phone call.

Over the sound of blood pounding in his ears, Pete could hear the phone – it was already ringing. He ordered his legs to go faster. They did, but they weren't very happy about it.

The ringing was louder now – just a few more steps to go. Pete reached for the phone and . . . the ringing stopped. He was too late!

He rested against the phone and tried to catch his breath. What now? Would the thieves call again or was that it?

Suddenly, he heard a noise – he wasn't alone in the phone box! There was something else in here, something *above* him! Pete looked up, but he caught only a glimpse of fur before something dropped on to his shoulders and shoved the cap down over his eyes.

'OI!' the captain cried, but then he heard the door open and felt a HUGE pair of hands pull him out of the phone box. These powerful hands lifted him as if he weighed no more than a rag doll (although, in fact, Peter Porker weighed more than any rag doll in recorded history). He was still in that vice-like grip when he felt the case being ripped from his trotter. For a few moments it felt like he was being frisked – then he was shoved backwards into the phone-box door, and he slumped to the ground. The thieves disappeared with a rustle of leaves.

Wasting no time, Pete scrabbled to pull the cap from over his eyes. He looked around quickly. In the distance, he could see two tiny figures swinging away through

the trees. Actually, one of them was tiny; the other looked pretty big, even from afar.

Tammy was shouting into his earphone. 'Are you OK, Pete? What's going on?'

'I'm OK,' he answered. Turning round, he saw a flat, rectangular object propped against the outside of the phone box. It was wrapped in brown paper. The captain carefully tore off one corner and peeked inside.

He smiled. 'And the *Mona Fleasa*'s looking pretty good, too!'

CHAPTER 4:

Mona's Makeover

The team rushed back to the National Primate Gallery. Their plan was to drop the painting off safely, and then monitor the radio for news of a sighting of two robbers covered in bright purple paint.

A burly baboon guard greeted them in the lobby. 'I'll take that,' he grunted, nodding at the wrapped painting.

Pete glanced at the guard's name-tag. 'Sorry, Bubbles. I'm handing this baby over to nobody except Pedalbin himself. Tell him we'll be waiting in Gallery 13, will you?'

The baboon lurched off to get his boss.

While Tammy tuned the radio in to the police wavelength, Pete carefully removed the brown paper and propped the painting against the wall. The PiPs all just looked at it in amazement.

It was smaller than Curly expected, but it was still incredible to be looking at the *Mona Fleasa* right in front of him.

'There it is,' Pete said, 'that famous, mysterious smile!'

'Pretty cool, eh, Bri?' Tammy elbowed the medic.

But Brian didn't answer. He was frowning as he looked at the picture. Before he could say anything, Tammy looked at her watch and announced, 'Well, in about twenty seconds, we'll have something to smile about too. That's when the timer is set to go off.'

'Hey, what's that sound?' asked Curly.

He was talking about the whirring noise that was coming from one of the many pockets in Pete's flightsuit. The captain pulled out a small round object with a dial on one side.

'That looks just like the paint bomb,' commented Brian helpfully. Then he blinked and cried, 'Hold on! That IS the paint bomb!'

Understanding smacked the PiPs about their heads like a wet kipper. The thieves must have taken the bomb out of the case and slipped it into Pete's pocket!

'It's going to explode!' cried Tammy. 'Chuck it out of the window!'

With a determined nod, Pete hurled the paint bomb towards the window. He had a good throwing arm and he hit the window dead-centre. Unfortunately, this was super-strong, reinforced glass – the window didn't break. The paint bomb struck it with a dull thud and bounced back into the room. It rolled across the floor, right towards the

Mona Fleasa.

Reacting on instinct alone, Pete leapt forward, throwing himself between the bomb and the masterpiece. Tammy did the same; so did Brian and so did Curly. All four pigs slammed into each other in mid-air, right as the paint bomb went off, POOF! A shower of bright purple paint slapped against them.

As they got back to their trotters, they all looked nervously at the painting. Had any of the purple paint landed on it?

Thankfully none had made it past the solid wall of pork that the pigs had put in its way – the painting was unharmed.

Pete grinned in relief and held up a trotter. 'High five!'

Tammy's trotter slapped into his. Unfortunately, the paint had not dried yet; as their two trotters slapped together in celebration, a purple splodge flew off. As if in slow motion, it sailed through the air and landed – PLOP! – right on the *Mona Fleasa*, just above her famous smile. The mysterious monkey had just grown a purple spot on her upper lip!

The PiPs goggled at it in horror.

'Don't worry!' cried Tammy, pulling out a crumpled tissue from her pocket. 'That'll come off, quick as a jiffy!'

She began to dab at the dot of purple paint. All this succeeded in doing was smearing it out into a line.

'Er, maybe if I spit on the tissue?' said Tammy hopefully.

But they all knew it would do no good. The priceless *Mona Fleasa* – the most famous painting in the world – now sported a purple moustache.

'Do you think anyone will notice?' asked Curly nervously.

Pete gulped. 'Not unless they look at it.'

When Pedalbin swept into the room minutes later and saw the four bright purple PiPs, he said nothing. He didn't need to – his arched eyebrow said everything.

'Where is my painting?' he demanded. 'And are there any disgusting smudge marks on it?'

Pete quickly positioned himself between the curator and the masterpiece. 'Which would you like first, Rob – the good news or the bad news?'

Pedalbin's eyes narrowed suspiciously. 'The bad.'

'OK, the bad news is . . . we've had a *tiny* bit of an accident with the *Mona Fleasa*,' Pete admitted.

The curator's eyes narrowed some more.

'And the good news?'

'Well . . . I think purple suits her!' said Pete, stepping aside so Pedalbin could see the painting.

In the sudden icy silence, all eyes were on Pedalbin. Curly had expected the colobus monkey to react badly. He'd imagined lots of screaming and leaping around and a few words that nice monkeys really shouldn't know. In fact, for several long seconds the curator just blinked and nodded slowly as he took in the damage to the world's most priceless masterpiece.

Then he went bananas.

In the hours that followed, there was a flurry of angry phone calls from Monkey Island to Pig Island. The matter quickly reached the top levels of government – soon everyone knew that the PiPs had ruined the greatest work of art in Animal

Paradise. A government minister angrily called the Chief Air Marshal of the PIAF (Pig Island Air Force), and in turn the Chief Air Marshal angrily called Peregrine at the PiPs base. Not being one to break the chain, Peregrine angrily called the PiPs, who were waiting by the parked SkyHogs.

'By going against orders, you've let the museum down,' the Wing Commander told them crossly, '*and* you've let art lovers everywhere down. But more than that, do you know who you've *really* let down?'

'Ourselves?' guessed Curly.

'No!' harrumphed Peregrine. 'You've let ME down! The Chief Air Marshal is so mad he's talking about getting rid of the PiPs altogether! In the meantime, the two governments have reached an agreement while they see if the *Mona Fleasa* can be restored.'

'What agreement's that?' asked Pete.

'If you're near a television, turn it to
Channel 3 now and you'll see,' answered the
Wing Commander.

Tammy's zappy new phone could get TV
channels, so the PiPs crowded round the
little screen to see the Monkey Island news.

The capuchin monkey newsreader was
saying, 'And finally . . . we've just heard
that the Pig Island Museum of Swine Art
is loaning its most famous work of art
to Monkey Island.' A photo of a statue
appeared behind the newsdesk. 'The

sculpture shows a mythological scene in which the piggy god of love, Pig's-Earos, fires an arrow of love at a young hog called Porcus. The exhibit goes on display at the National Primate Gallery tomorrow.'

When Tammy clicked the news off, Peregrine was waiting on the radio. 'If it turns out that the *Mona* can't be restored, the deal is that Monkey Island will get to *keep* this priceless art treasure from Pig Island,' he said. 'And if that happens, we can all wave our jobs goodbye.'

Pete grabbed the radio. 'Peregrine, who's bringing the sculpture here?'

'My orders are to deliver it personally,' answered the Wing Commander. 'And I want you all to remain there until I arrive so you can help unload . . . Why do you ask?'

'There's this idea I want to run past you.' Pete winked at the other PiPs and carried the radio out of earshot.

CHAPTER 5:

Monkey Business

Peregrine still didn't look very happy
when he landed the cargo plane outside
the National Primate Gallery. His huge
moustache twitched in agitation as he
watched Tammy and Curly open the plane's
cargo doors and wheel out a large crate
into the car park.

Pete joined the Wing Commander.
'Thanks for doing this, Peregrine,' he said
quietly.

Peregrine glared. 'As far as the Pig Island
government knows, I have followed orders
and delivered the statue. Only Lola and I

know about this little plan of yours. If it doesn't work, you know what will happen? Our whole agency will be for the chop!'

Pete just grinned. 'Trust me, Wing Commander!' He followed the crate as the others pushed it inside. 'Have a safe flight home,' he called over his shoulder.

As Peregrine climbed back into the cargo plane, he nibbled nervously on a chocolate biccie. Meanwhile, the rest of the PiPs wheeled the crate to one of the museum's store rooms and Tammy set about opening it with a crowbar. Curly waited, ready to see the famous piggy sculpture. He was a bit surprised to see nothing inside the crate but a big bucket and several packets of dry powder.

'There's no sculpture,' Brian said, sounding confused. 'What's going on?'

'We're the Pigs in Planes,' Pete answered proudly. 'No one makes monkeys of us!

That's why I asked Peregrine to keep the
real sculpture at Snout Island.'

Brian went pale. 'Er . . . so we've
disobeyed a direct PIAF order?'

'Yup!' said Pete. 'Because if those thieves
think the statue's here, I *know* they'll try to
steal it. And when they do, there'll be a big
surprise waiting for them!' He put a trotter
on Curly's shoulder. 'The stuff in those
packets is plaster. You and I, young Curly,

are going to be living sculptures. We'll BE
the statue they try to steal!'

Curly's eyes were big. 'What will I have to
do?'

Pete smiled. 'Absolutely nothing.'

The trainee PiP nodded eagerly. 'I can do
that!'

The team got to work. Tammy was in
charge of mixing up the plaster in the
gigantic bucket. Brian had given her exact
measurements to make it the right thickness.

'The trick is getting it
hard enough for them
to seem like statues,' he
explained, 'but soft enough
for them to break free.'

Meanwhile Brian's job
was to arrange Pete and
Curly into the right
pose. Curly had already
changed into a toga.

'What about my costume?' asked Pete.

'Oops, sorry!' said Brian. He handed the captain a pair of fake wings, along with a small quiver of arrows. 'Put these on.'

'That's not the whole costume, is it?'

'No, of course not!' chuckled Brian. 'Here – wear this headband too.'

Pete shrugged – he wasn't a shy pig. Moments later he had unzipped his flightsuit and stood ready and waiting in his bright red Speedio trunks.

Tammy was still stirring the plaster mix with a stick.

'Have you put on a bit of weight, Pete?' she asked.

'I have,' beamed Pete happily. 'Thanks for noticing.'

Tammy paused, trying to remember how many scoops of plaster she still needed to put in – was it four or five? She shrugged and put six in. Then she put two more in for good luck.

Meanwhile Pete had the wings on, and now he balanced on one trotter and held the bow and arrow out in an exact copy of the god in *Earos and Porcus*.

'Stay still while we get this on you,' instructed Brian, as he slapped wet plaster on to the captain.

As the plaster covered more and more of his body, Pete could feel it drying and hardening. Soon it was no effort to keep his body in position because the plaster held him in place. Brian covered the captain's face last of all, taking care to leave eyeholes and breathing holes for the mouth and nose.

'That looks brilliant – just like a real statue!' said Tammy.

Brian began to apply plaster to Curly, who had assumed his statue's pose, arching his back in shock and gripping one side of his bum, which had an arrow poking out of it.

Tammy pointed at it. 'What a cheek!' she said, laughing. She realized that she'd lost count of the number of scoops again. With a shrug, she emptied the rest of the packet into the water.

At last, Brian was done. He stepped back and looked at his work. He nodded with satisfaction – the two pigs looked just like the famous sculpture. Pete was standing on one leg and holding his bow in one outstretched arm.

'Are you sure we'll be able to break out of this plaster?' asked Pete in a muffled voice. 'It feels pretty solid to me.'

'You'll have no problem,' replied Brian. 'I checked the measurements I gave Tammy twice! Now we just have to get you to the Special Exhibition Hall. And then we wait . . .'

It was dark by the time Tammy and Brian had positioned the new sculpture in the Special Exhibition Hall. Pedalbin had agreed that the pigs could take care of the security themselves. The baboon guards would keep away from this part of the museum.

'There's a guards' room with a CCTV link direct to this hall,' said Tammy. 'We'll wait in there and watch everything.'

She and Brian trotted off, leaving the two 'statues' in the silence of the dark gallery. It wasn't long before Curly broke the silence:

'I've got an itchy snout,' he whispered.

Time passed, and then Curly whispered
again:

'I think I need a wee.'

More time passed, then the trainee
whispered again:

'Yes, I definitely need a wee.'

Some more time passed, then:

'Actually I'm hungry. I fancy some popcorn.'

Even more time passed. Curly whispered:

'I'm *bored*. How long have we been here anyway?'

Pete was facing the clock on the wall. 'Three and a half minutes,' he said, and he thought to himself, *This is going to be a long, long night.*

CHAPTER 6:

Gilbo and George

Pete wasn't wrong. It was a long night for
Tammy in the guards' room too.

She sat and stared at the CCTV screen.
She had almost eaten her own body weight
in crisps. 'BOR-ing!' she burped. 'This makes
watching plaster dry look like a carnival.'

Brian didn't answer. His snout was buried
in a book – *The Ultimate Art Lovers' Guide to
Great Art*. He had bookmarked several pages
with little sticky notes. Occasionally he
leaned forward and put his eyes right up to
the book. At the moment he was staring at
the page with a picture of the *Mona Fleasa*

and he was scribbling furiously in a little notepad.

Tammy pointed to the screen. 'Hey, look – a fly just landed on the camera lens. That's the most exciting thing that's happened in two hours!'

Brian didn't even look up from his notes.

Frozen inside the plaster, Pete could hear Curly softly snoring. He was beginning to wonder if this was such a good idea, when suddenly he heard another sound. It came from above – a clunking noise and then the sound of the wind outside.

'Psst, Curly!' he whispered. 'Wake up.'

Curly made a startled snuffling sound inside the statue. 'Erm, I wasn't asleep. I was just resting my eyes,' he lied.

'Just keep quiet,' said Pete. 'Something's happening.'

More sounds came from above, but

because of the plaster Pete couldn't lift his head and see what was going on.

Suddenly a low voice echoed round the gallery. 'Just a little to the left.'

Pete instantly recognized the voice – the one on the other end of the line at the handover!

'OK, Gilbo,' came a second, squeakier voice.

'How many times have I told you not to use my name on a job,' hissed the first.

'George is sorry, Gilbo!' The second voice was so squeaky it sounded almost child-like to Pete.

'Just stop talking and lower me a touch more,' snarled the one called Gilbo.

The speaker came into Pete's line of vision – a skinny chimpanzee wearing a bowler hat and a black overcoat. A rope was tied round his waist and Pete guessed that the owner of the second voice – George –

was lowering Gilbo into the gallery from the skylight.

The chimpanzee carried a second rope and a harness in his furry hands. Working quickly, he began to strap the harness around Pete and Curly.

After a couple of minutes, Gilbo hissed up to his accomplice. 'OK, George. Pull!'

The second rope began to stretch taut, the leather straps of the harness tightened, and slowly Pete and Curly began to rise into the air. Pete wondered what sort of technology they were using to winch them up – he couldn't hear the sound of any machinery.

When they were about halfway up, they swayed in mid-air and Pete got a better view of what was above them. The entire frame of the skylight had been removed, and a single figure filled the gap. George.

It was clear that George didn't need the help of any gadgets or lifting machinery. He was the biggest gorilla Pete had ever set eyes on. Like his partner, the chimpanzee, George was wearing a bowler hat and black overcoat. The difference was that his hat perched on his huge head like a doll's, and he looked as if he'd burst out of his XXXL coat if he decided to flex his chest muscles. His gigantic hands hauled on the rope as if the two pigs weighed no more than squirrel monkeys.

George stuck out his bottom
lip as he got a better look at the
statue. 'George doesn't think this
one much good,' he mumbled.
'Not like the picture of the nice
Smiley Lady . . .'

'Leave the thinking to me,
George!' snapped Gilbo. 'You
just do the grunt work and give
your hazelnut-sized
brain a rest.'

★ ★ ★

In the CCTV security room, Tammy was struggling to keep her eyes open. How many hours could you just sit and look at Pete and Curly pretending to be statues? It didn't help that Brian was still tutting over his book and scribbling notes.

Suddenly, a blobby shape appeared on the screen.

'That fly's back again,' murmured Tammy sleepily. 'That's the third or fourth time now.'

She watched the fly walk forward a little, wave its front legs about in that yucky fly way, then walk forward some more.

'Hey, that's what it did last time,' said Tammy. '*And* the time before that . . . Wait a minute!' She sat forward, staring intently at the screen. The fly completed a loop, then flew off. 'That's *exactly* the same! How could that happen, unless . . .'

Brian looked up from his book. 'Tammy

. . . There's something very wrong here.'

'You've got that right!' cried Tammy. 'What we're watching on that screen isn't live footage! It's a *recording*!' She leapt up. 'Come on! We've got to go and check on Pete and Curly!'

She charged out of the door and Brian could do nothing but follow. When he caught up, Tammy had already reached the Special Exhibition Hall. Everything looked completely normal . . . except there was no sign whatsoever of Pete and Curly. The statue had disappeared!

'Now we don't know *who* did it, *when* they did it, or *how*,' Tammy said, looking around frantically. 'This explains why no one saw them steal the *Mona Fleasa* either.'

'Tammy, listen, there's something else I need to tell you!' said Brian urgently.

'What?' asked the mechanic, hunting around the room for clues.

'It's probably best if I just show you . . .' he replied.

A few minutes later the two pigs were standing outside the art restoration studio, where Pedalbin had taken the *Mona Fleasa*.

'Shouldn't we be looking for Pete and Curly?' asked Tammy.

'We don't even know where to begin,' said Brian. 'And this won't take long. It's something you *need* to see.'

The door was locked but that didn't stop Tammy – she pulled out a hairpin and quickly picked the lock. Inside the studio, there were shelves and shelves of special cleaning fluids. The *Mona Fleasa* lay face-up on a table.

'Look at it carefully,' said Brian. 'Notice anything odd?'

Tammy frowned. 'Apart from the purple moustache?'

'No, in the background . . . I *thought* there

was something wrong when we first got the painting back, but I couldn't quite put my trotter on it.' Brian picked up a magnifying glass and held it over part of the painting. 'Look here.'

Tammy peered through the lens. 'It looks like a load of trees and bushes in the background.'

'Yes,' cried Brian, 'but one of those trees *shouldn't* be there!' He waved his book around excitedly. 'It's not in the book!'

Tammy blinked. 'So . . . someone has painted on top of the world's most famous picture?'

Brian shook his head. 'No! I think this isn't the real *Mona Fleasa*. It's a forgery! Whoever did it made a fantastic copy, but they added a new detail!'

'Why?' asked Tammy.

'I think it's a hidden message. Look at the type of tree . . . ' Brian pointed at the magnifying glass. 'It's a *monkey-puzzle tree*. Whoever put it there was trying to send a message that there's a puzzle to work out. If we solve it, it might

even help us find Pete and Curly.'

'Complicated way of sending a message,' muttered Tammy. 'Couldn't they just have texted?'

'That's not all!' Brian moved his magnifying glass to another part of the painting's background where a distant band of peasants was walking along. 'Look at this monkey at the front.'

'The one with the blue guitar?'

'Yes, but he isn't supposed to have a guitar!' cried Brian, holding open the book for Tammy to see. 'And look at the peasant behind him – she isn't supposed to have her eyes shut or her hands over her ears!'

Again Tammy checked the book and saw that Brian was right. 'So what does it mean?' she asked.

Brian was ready with an answer. 'I think the fact that the guitar is blue is important,' he said. 'There's a famous painting with a *blue* guitar – it's here in this museum! I think someone has painted these clues telling us to look at other paintings in the gallery!'

He rushed towards the door.

'Let me guess,' said Tammy. 'We're going to play another game of Spot the Difference?'

CHAPTER 7:

Picture Puzzles

Gilbo and George wheeled the piggy statue
into a large, dark hall. Actually, the gorilla
did all the work, while the chimp hopped
about, gave orders and called George a
'stupid, slope-browed ape' and other not-
very-nice names.

In fact, George had done all the work the
whole way here. He had lowered the piggy
statue to the ground outside the museum,
and he had lifted it into the back of the
waiting van. After a short drive, George
was the one who'd unloaded the statue
and wheeled it inside on a trolley. Unable

to turn his neck and get a better view, Pete
hadn't managed to see much, but one thing
was clear – this was a huge mansion. He
was pretty sure that Gilbo and George
weren't its owners; they were probably just
the hired muscle.

They went through room after room,
down in a lift, and then finally came to
a large, gloomy hall. The gorilla lifted
the statue off the trolley and set it down.
Then he took a step back and stared at the
sculpture.

'George doesn't like it,' he said at last.
'Too ugly.'

'Well thank you, Professor George from
the University of *Duh-Can-I-Have-a-Banana*!'
snapped Gilbo. 'You're not paid to think!
Mrs Van Housen pays you to pick heavy
things up and put them down in different
places. She pays ME to think!'

'Actually I pay you to do what you're

told,' said a thin voice from the back of the room. A small figure emerged into the light. She was a little golden tamarin monkey. Her hair was swept high in an immaculate bouffant and her expensive designer clothes perfectly matched her orange fur. She carried a banana in one dainty hand.

'Yes, of course, Mrs Van Housen,' grovelled Gilbo, whisking off his bowler hat and clasping it in both hands.

The tamarin monkey gave a sweet smile that was actually a bit scary. She approached Pete and Curly.

'So this is the best work of art Pig Island has to offer?' She walked slowly around the 'statue', her heels clacking like lightning on the marble floor. She broke off a piece of banana and popped it into her mouth, chewing carefully. When she had finished, she simply dropped the banana skin on to the floor, safe in the knowledge that one of her many servants would have to pick it up.

'This sculpture is hideous!' she declared at last. 'It belongs in a sty, not a serious art collection.'

Inside the statue, Pete had to remind himself that statues weren't supposed to talk – otherwise he'd give this cheeky monkey a piece of his mind!

Mrs Van Housen turned on her high heels and began to walk away. 'You need not add this to the Special Collection,' she said over her shoulder. 'Get the other pieces ready for tonight's exhibition, then you can come back and dispose of this monstrosity.'

In the dark halls of the National Primate Gallery, Tammy and Brian were standing in front of another painting. Pigasso had painted this on one of his trips to Monkey Island; it showed a big mandrill monkey sitting in an alley and playing a blue guitar.

'It's from Pigasso's famous Blue Bum Period,' explained Brian, 'when he painted lots of pictures of blue-bottomed mandrills.'

'Er, why?' asked Tammy.

'Some art historians think he used blue to capture a mood of quiet sadness. Others reckon he bought too much blue paint on sale, so he wanted to use it up.'

Brian studied the copy in his art book for a few moments, then he looked up at the painting. He pointed to a building in the picture's background.

'There's supposed to be a church tower here,' he said, 'but there *isn't* meant to be a bell in it! And what's that sticking out of the bell?'

Tammy leaned in towards the canvas. 'Looks like an arrow.'

Brian was getting excited – he knew that they were on to something. He kept on examining the picture. Finally, he waved a trotter around one small patch of shadows. 'What does this bit look like to you?'

Tammy squinted. 'Maybe the outline of a truck or a van or something?'

'That's it – a van!' Brian looked for a few minutes more, but he could find nothing else out of place.

Tammy was struggling to share his excitement. 'I just don't get what it all means!' she said.

Brian reminded her of the other clue in the *Mona* – the peasant with her eyes closed and her hands over her ears. 'I think that's a clue to a different painting!' he said, and he led Tammy to another famous work.

This one was called *See No Evil, Hear No Evil, Speak No Evil*, and it showed a row of three monkeys. The first was covering its eyes, the second its ears, and the third had a hand clamped over its mouth.

'Wonder why they didn't put *Smell No Evil* in there?' commented Tammy.

Again Brian consulted his art book before concentrating on the painting's background, which showed forest on one side and farmland on the other.

After a few minutes he pointed at one area and cried, 'There! See the little house, next to the farm? That's not supposed to be there! Nor is that little chicken in front of the house!'

Tammy thought it over. 'OK, let's say there *are* forgeries in the museum with clues painted in them. The question is, why? What do they mean?'

'Well,' said Brian thoughtfully, 'we've got an arrow and a bell. Then there was a van. And in this picture there's a house and a chicken. It must mean something.'

Tammy's eyes lit up. 'Maybe a HEN with a bow and ARROW did the crime? She took the paintings in a VAN to her HOUSE?'

'What about the bell?' asked Brian.

Tammy thought for a moment. 'Maybe her van had a BELL instead of a horn?'

Brian shook his head slowly. 'It doesn't sound very likely,' he said. 'But maybe the letters of the words make a scrambled message?'

He opened his notepad and neatly wrote:

ARROW BELL VAN HOUSE HEN

He spent a couple of minutes rearranging the letters to see what other words they might make.

'Well?' said Tammy. 'What have you got?'

Brian looked up. 'SHAVE HORN UNREAL ELBOW.'

'Great!' said Tammy. 'That makes a lot more sense!'

Brian flipped the pad shut. 'What can it mean then? Arrow, bell, van, house, hen . . .?'

'There's someone who may know,' said Tammy, 'and I bet he's still in the museum working late.'

Brian nodded. 'Pedalbin.'

Pete and Curly had a problem.

The plan had been simple enough – once they were taken to the thieves' lair, they would break out of the plaster as soon as they were alone.

Well, they were alone now, but the rest of

the plan had gone a bit wrong. The plaster wouldn't crack, no matter how hard they tried to move their arms and legs – and they tried *really* hard. They were trapped.

'Do you think Brian and Tammy got the recipe wrong?' asked Curly.

'It looks like it. But we need to do something before those two primates get back,' said Pete. He searched his brain for ideas, but found it empty. It was time to rely on his gut instead.

Pete sucked in air through his nostrils and filled his chest and tummy. An instant later, he blew all the air out, then sucked in more. He kept on doing this, inflating and deflating his big tummy until it took on a life of its own. It began to roll like the swell of the sea, and like the sea it was soon an unstoppable force.

Pete was balanced on only one foot, and now he began to sway in time to the

uncontrolled rolling of his stomach. He
rocked backwards and forwards, backwards
and forwards, each time just a little bit
further until . . . gravity kicked in and he
went crashing to the floor.

Instantly the plaster cast
cracked open. Digging his trotters into the
crack, Pete pulled the rest of the plaster off.
He was still covered in white dust, but he
was free! He reached round and scratched

himself right between the shoulders.

'I've been waiting hours to do that!'

Next he tried to get Curly free, but it was impossible. Pete pushed and pulled and hit it, but the plaster around the trainee was as hard as rock.

'We'll have to cut you out of there,' Pete said. 'And until we find something to do that, I'm going to have to pull you along.'

The captain tilted Curly back and started dragging him, past numerous paintings and sculptures. Pete was no great art lover, but he couldn't help thinking that some of these works looked awfully familiar.

At one point he heard footsteps from round the corner at the far end of the room. Quickly Pete set Curly upright, assumed the Earos statue pose again and froze.

He was just in time. Moments later Gilbo the chimpanzee came round the corner. He stopped and looked at the sculpture suspiciously – was that where they had left it? But then he just shrugged, lifted another painting off the wall, and went back the way he had come.

When the coast was clear, Pete continued to pull Curly along. At last they came to the end of the long room. Pete turned left and followed the corridor to a staircase and a closed door.

'Which way now?' Pete wondered.

'Um, hard to say,' answered Curly. 'I can only see the ceiling from this angle.'

Pete set the trainee back upright so he could see both options.

'Shouldn't we take the stairs?' said Curly. 'We're in an underground part of the mansion, right?'

But Pete wasn't so sure. 'This is all too easy,' he said. 'We haven't come across any security measures yet, but they *must* have some for all those works of art. I'll bet one

of these ways out is booby-trapped.' He
thought for a moment. 'And my gut tells me
. . . it's the stairs!'

'OK, Pete.' Curly would have shrugged if
he wasn't encased in rock-hard plaster.

Pete pushed open the door. It was low
and he had to bend down as he dragged
Curly through it, into an empty white
room. There was another door on the far
side of the room, but this had no handle.
Pete pushed it, but the door didn't
budge.

He turned to go back the way they
had come, but the door they'd just

entered through wouldn't open from the inside either. They were stuck in here.

'What's that whirring noise?' asked Curly.

Pete looked around but saw nothing. He looked up at the ceiling. He rubbed his eyes and looked again. It almost looked as if the ceiling was moving lower and lower. There was a good reason for this – the ceiling WAS moving lower and lower.

'This room is the booby-trap!' he cried. If they didn't get out of here, they were going to get squashed flatter than a thin-crust pizza with extra bacon.

CHAPTER 8:

Trapped!

As they walked through the dark halls of the museum, Brian muttered the clues under his breath. 'Bell, House, Hen, Van, Arrow ... Arrow, Bell, Van, House, Hen.'

The light in the curator's office was still on. Tammy and Brian quickened their step, but as they approached, they could hear Pedalbin's voice through the partly open door.

'He's on the phone,' whispered Tammy.

'Yes, yes, of course it is a *dreadful* work of art,' Pedalbin was saying, 'but the nitwits of Pig Island consider it to be a masterpiece.'

Tammy and Brian stopped – Pedalbin was talking about the statue of *Earos and Porcus*. They listened on, as the curator said, 'Yes, yes, of course, Mrs Van Housen.'

Brian had been about to push the door open, but he stopped. His eyes widened. 'Did he just say "Van Housen"?' he whispered to Tammy.

Tammy nodded. 'So?'

'VAN Housen? Van HOUSE HEN! The clues in the paintings!'

Tammy wasn't convinced. 'Probably just a coincidence,' she hissed. 'Anyway, it doesn't explain the ARROW and the BELL, does it?'

She was reaching out for the door handle when Pedalbin's voice spoke out again. 'Yes, of course. I'll be there soon, Arabelle.'

This time Tammy froze. 'Arabelle?' she whispered. 'ARROW BELL!'

Understanding dawned on both pigs at the same moment. The clues in the paintings were for someone's name – Arrow, Bell, Van, House, Hen – *Arabelle Van Housen*! What's more, it seemed the curator of the art gallery knew her!

The two pigs looked at each other with wide eyes, unsure what to do now. But they made up their minds as soon as they heard

Pedalbin's next words: 'Don't worry about the PiPs, Mrs Van Housen. My baboons will deal with them while I come to the mansion.'

Tammy's eyes widened in shock – Pedalbin was in on it! Slowly the pigs turned and began to tiptoe away, hoping they hadn't been noticed. If they could just get out of here, they'd be able to radio PiPs HQ and tell Lola everything.

Suddenly they heard the sound of claws on marble. They looked up and saw four of the museum's fearsome security baboons charging towards them.

'Got any ideas?' wailed Tammy.

'Yes,' said Brian. 'Run!'

It wasn't the medic's best plan ever, but it was the only option. The pigs pelted in the opposite direction as fast as their trotters could carry them. They could hear the horrible grunts of the baboons behind them.

'This way!' shouted Brian,
skidding round a corner and
into the modern art wing.

Tammy followed him, but the
pigs quickly realized something
– with the exit closed and no
time to pick the lock, this part of
the museum was a dead end!

Brian raced to the alarm
panel on the wall and elbowed
the glass. Immediately, a siren
went off and steel shutters
dropped down over all the doors

and windows with a metallic CLANG!

'It's the security system,' explained Brian. 'Pedalbin told me that the shutters are on a timelock – they'll stay down for twenty minutes. After that, the baboons will be able to get in.'

Tammy looked around. 'Great, Bri – but how are *we* going to get *out*?'

Meanwhile, at the mansion of Mrs Van Housen, the ceiling of the booby-trapped room continued to drop lower and lower.

Pete tried shoulder-charging the door they'd just come through, but it was no good. Thinking fast, he picked Curly up, holding the trainee lengthways.

'Er, what are you doing?' Curly asked.

'Using you as a battering-ram,' said the captain, and he ran at the door.

Curly's plaster-covered head struck the door hard – *THWOCK!* – but with no effect. Pete stood Curly back up, and tried to think of another plan. The ceiling was getting nearer and nearer. Pete couldn't stand upright now. If this continued, the ceiling would splat them like two bugs – gigantic pink ones.

Suddenly, the whirr of the hidden mechanism changed to a whine – the ceiling had reached the top of Curly's head. It was pressing down with a lot of force, but the cast around Curly's body was strong enough to withstand it. But who knew for how long? Tiny cracks were already beginning to appear in the plaster.

'I don't like this!' wailed Curly.

'What's to like?' answered Pete, looking around frantically. If only there was something in the room he could pry open the door with. Then he remembered the quiver of arrows over his back! He pulled one out and began to work at the door's crack with the sharp arrowhead. It took a while, but finally he was able to lever the door open. He could escape, but with Curly stuck in a rock-hard plaster cast and held in place by the force of an entire ceiling pressing down on him, there was no chance to rescue the young pig.

'There must be an off-switch somewhere outside the room,' Pete said. 'I'm going to find it.'

'What should I do?' cried Curly.

This was an easy one. 'You stay here!' cried Pete, bending down and nipping through the door.

The first thing Tammy tried to do was call PiPs HQ for help.

'No reception,' she said angrily. 'Something must be blocking the signal!'

Brian pointed up at the glass dome in the middle of the ceiling high above them.

'That's our exit!' he said. 'We just need to find a way to get up there.'

Tammy shook her head. 'We'll never be able to reach it.' But then her eye fell on the art installation with all the bits of wood and rubbish, with a bike on top. She ran over to it.

'Don't touch that!' shouted Brian. 'That piece is called *Eternal Rubbish Skip of Time*. It's a leading example of the Dustbin School of Art.'

'It's *perfect*,' grinned Tammy.

Brian paused. 'Really? You like it?'

'I love it!' said Tammy. 'And I REALLY love what it's going to be!'

She whipped out a spanner and screwdriver from her top pocket. 'Remember those sketches of flying-machines by Leo Nardo . . .?'

As the door to the booby-trapped room swung shut behind him, Pete looked around for some sort of control box. All he could see was one panel with lots of buttons, but it was right next to the door at the top of the staircase. Pete raced towards it, taking the steps two at a time.

His bare trotters clacked on the wooden stairs. But then, when he was halfway up, suddenly there was another sound – more of a CLICK than a CLACK!

Pete just had time to murmur, 'Uh-OH!' before the stairs flattened out underneath him, turning into a slide. The stairs were booby-trapped too, which hardly seemed fair! Unable to keep his balance, Pete fell forward and started slipping down the slope.

He tumbled down trotters-first, straight through a trapdoor, which had opened up at the bottom of the staircase to reveal a narrow chute. Looking down, Pete caught a glimpse of something at the bottom of the shaft – several sharp somethings, glittering in

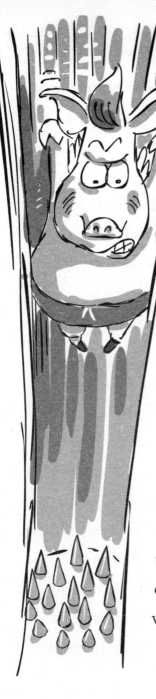

the dark. Spikes! This booby-trap was even worse than the one in the room!

However, this particular trap had been designed for someone a bit less ... *full-figured* than Peter Porker. About halfway down the chute he came to a halt. His large tummy was wedged against the sides.

Pete gasped in relief. He knew his gut instinct to eat an extra helping of chips at every meal would pay off someday. Now all he had to do

was climb out of here and rescue Curly
before the trainee was squashed flatter than
a savoury pancake with ham filling . . .

CHAPTER 9:

The Soaring Genius of Leo Nardo

Once Brian got past his horror at the idea of dismantling a famous work of modern art, he and Tammy worked quickly. They were a good team – he was an all-round genius and she was a brilliant mechanic. Brian assembled some rotor blades from plywood, while Tammy worked on the mechanism for turning them round and round. Both pigs had suggestions for how to improve Leo's original design.

'When this mission's over, we'll put this work of art back exactly as it was,' said Brian. 'Right?'

Tammy shrugged as she attached the mechanism to the bike frame. 'You mean, chuck it in a corner any old way? Yeah, we can do that.' She glanced nervously at her watch. 'Anyway, the shutters will go back up in a couple of minutes,' she said. 'If those baboons get in before we get this baby off the ground, there won't BE an end to this mission. At least, not a happy one . . .'

She tightened up the last of the struts. 'It's ready for a test run.'

Brian glanced nervously at the shutters. 'OK, but we haven't got long.'

Quickly Tammy hopped on to the bike seat and began to pedal. As the chain whirred round, the rotor blades did too, becoming a blur over Tammy's head.

'Faster!' cried Brian.

Tammy pedalled harder and slowly the flying-machine began to wobble up into the air.

'It's working!' cried Brian. His surprised joy lasted for roughly 1.6 seconds, and then there was a CLICK and the steel shutters began to rise.

The four beefy baboons charged into the room. Their muzzles all displayed scary-looking teeth, and it didn't bear thinking what their long, powerful arms could do to a couple of pigs.

But the homemade flying-machine was hovering at head height now. 'Jump on!' shouted Tammy. Brian leapt up and grabbed the bike frame with one trotter. It dipped for a moment, but then Tammy pedalled even faster and the machine wobbled higher.

By the time the first baboon reached them, Brian's feet were just out of its hairy reach. Grunting in anger, the guard leapt high. Its hand grazed Brian's trotter, but it couldn't quite grab him.

Brian looked down at the cluster of

furious baboons.
'So long, monkeys!'
he yelled. Then he
realized they weren't
going any higher.
'Er . . . Tammy,
can you pedal a bit
faster, please?'

'This isn't very easy,
you know!' snapped
Tammy. The bike
chain whizzed around,
but they continued
only to hover in the
air. Below them one
of the baboons was
starting to clamber on
to another's shoulders.

An idea hit Brian –
he could lighten the
load! With his spare

trotter he pulled out a huge book from the special book-carrying pocket he'd sewn into his flightsuit. 'Farewell, *Pop-Up History of Art, Volume 1*,' he said sadly. He threw the giant book down at the baboons.

One of the guards swatted it away easily, but they weren't so lucky with *Volume 2*. This struck a baboon on the head and knocked him out cold.

'That's better!' cried Tammy. The flying-machine was heading up again, out of reach of the enraged security guards. It spiralled around the room, picking up speed in tighter and tighter circles as it neared the glass dome in the ceiling.

'Watch out, we're going through!' cried Tammy.

An instant later they struck the glass. It shattered into a thousand pieces, which rained down into the gallery as the two pigs flew out into the moonlit night. Still

pedalling for all she was worth, Tammy glanced down and saw a knot of baboons guarding the parked SkyHogs.

Brian pulled out his radio. 'We MUST be able to get reception from up here!' he cried.

Moments later he was talking to Lola. 'Quick! We need an address in Simian City for someone called Arabelle Van Housen.'

'Roger that, Bri,' she replied.

It took the PiPs radio operator only a few seconds to pull up the information on her computer and report back. 'She's incredibly rich. She lives in a massive mansion in the hills to the north.' Lola gave them the address and then signed off.

Tammy turned the flying-machine north towards the biggest house on the biggest hill.

With his radio tucked away, Brian could hold on with both trotters. Even then, his arms were beginning to ache. 'Wonder how Pete and Curly are getting on?' he said.

Tammy pedalled on. 'You know Pete . . .
He's probably already solved the case and is
putting his trotters up.'

Brian said nothing. He had a bad feeling
that this case might not be quite so easy.

It took Pete a long time to climb out of the
booby-trap pit, sticking his elbows out wide
and wiggling upwards, while kicking with
his back trotters against the sides. Finally he
was able to reach up and take hold of the
trapdoor's edge. Gritting his teeth, he pulled
with all his might. It wasn't easy to haul
such a weight – he knew he should have
listened to his gut instinct and not eaten an
extra helping of chips at every meal.

Finally, he clambered out. But there was
no time to catch his breath.

'Curly!' he shouted, rushing back towards
the door into the little white room. But
when he burst in, he saw that the ceiling

was back up where it belonged, at the top of the room. As for Curly, apart from a scattering of plaster dust on the floor, there was no sign of the trainee pig whatsoever.

Pete shook a trotter in fury. 'If they've hurt a single bristle on that boy's head . . .'

In fact, Curly had *not* been crushed flat; nor had he been grabbed by Mrs Van Housen's henchmen. He was actually drinking a cup of tea. (Not that his situation was perfect – for one thing, the tea was a bit milky.) He was also looking at a skinny little spider monkey, who said his name was Vincent.

This was how Curly had met the spider monkey: back in the booby-trapped room, the cracks in the young pig's plaster cast had been getting bigger and bigger under the pressure of the ceiling. It had been about to burst when someone threw a switch outside the door on the far side of the room. The ceiling stopped, then it began to go back up. Moments later the door opened and a little furry head looked in.

Vincent wasn't a very big monkey, and it took all his strength to pull Curly back out through the door, which he had propped open.

'Wait!' cried Curly. 'I need to find my friend! He went back the other way! He was going up the stairs for help.'

Still dragging the plastered pig, Vincent giggled nervously. 'Forget him,' he said. 'If he went that way, there's nothing you can do for him.'

The little monkey had pulled Curly back along the corridor, past the gallery room and into a cluttered artist's studio, where he'd finally cut the trainee out of his plaster cast.

'Thanks,' said Curly, looking around as he stretched his arms and legs. The studio was full of artist's stuff – paints, pots, brushes, easels, empty frames, canvases – and the walls were covered in half-finished sketches. It was clear that Vincent was a talented artist.

'May I ask you a question?' said Curly, sipping his tea. 'What's going on here?'

Vincent chewed the tip of his tail nervously. 'I'm an artist,' he began, 'but I'm not very good at thinking of things to

paint. I'm good at copying other paintings though! That's why they keep me here and bring me works to copy.'

'You mean you make forgeries?' asked Curly.

Vincent giggled again and bobbled his head forward. 'Loads of them! They bring them from the National Primate Gallery and I make copies. Then they secretly send the fake back to the museum and keep the original. It was OK at first, but then I got fed up. I tried to leave but Mrs Van Housen's baboons just brought me back. I'm a prisoner here!' He grinned slyly at Curly. 'That's why I started putting clues in the paintings, so someone could come and rescue me. And here you are!' Disappointment flashed across the monkey's little face. 'Hmm. Hold on though – I *rescued* you! What are you doing here?'

'Me and my friends belong to the Pigs

in Planes — Animal Paradise's best crime-fighting unit,' Curly answered. 'We're here to solve this robbery, and we'll help you too.'

Vincent let out an excited giggle.

Curly didn't know anything about the clues in Vincent's paintings but there was still something that didn't make sense to him. 'What about the *Mona Fleasa*? Why didn't they just return a fake of that in secret, too? Why did they ask for a ransom?'

Vincent plucked a flea from his own fur and popped it into his mouth. 'Simple. The police interrupted the robbery and almost caught them. Gilbo and George got away, but it meant there was no chance to return the painting in secret. They had to go through with the whole ransom idea.' The monkey giggled. 'Mrs Van Housen doesn't need the money, that's for sure!'

Curly's mind was racing. He wished Pete was here — the captain would know what to do. 'We just need to get out of here,' he said. 'Then I'll call my commanding officer at PiPs HQ.'

Vincent's tail waved anxiously. 'There's no time for that!' he cried. 'Follow me!' The little monkey led Curly out of the studio and through the winding maze of hallways and corridors.

'They think I'm harmless,' he whispered. 'No one cares if I roam the mansion. It's when I try to leave the place that they get all upset.'

They rode a service lift upstairs and Vincent steered Curly to a window. The young pig looked down and saw dozens of cars pulling up in front of the mansion. A number of monkeys and apes – all stylishly dressed in black – were getting out. Uniformed baboons guided them to the entrance.

'Mrs Van Housen has invited everyone in

the Simian City art world to her mansion tonight,' hissed Vincent. 'She's got a special presentation in mind!'

Curly didn't like the sound of that. 'Show me,' he said.

'OK, walk this way!' answered Vincent, and he scurried off, knuckles dragging along the floor.

Curly knew what Pete would say in response to that, but of course the PiPs captain was not here; had he been caught in another of the mansion's terrible traps . . . or had something even *worse* happened?

And so, at the same moment that Pete was doing exactly the same thing in a different part of the mansion, Curly shook a trotter in fury: 'If they've hurt a bristle on my hero's head . . .'

CHAPTER 10:

The Naked Truth

There was an excited buzz in the air in the mansion's main hall. The art critics and collectors of Monkey Island, seated in rows of wooden chairs, were all wondering why they had been invited here.

They fell silent when a petite golden tamarin monkey stood to address them.

'Ladies and gentlemonkeys,' she began. 'I am Arabelle Van Housen. Welcome to the most important event in Animal Paradise's art history!'

She clapped her hands and baboon guards pulled back plush red velvet curtains to reveal various works of art around the hall. The crowd gasped: they were looking at some of the most famous paintings in the world.

'These copies are superb!' marvelled an elderly gibbon.

Mrs Van Housen fixed him with a golden eye. 'These are NOT copies, sir!' she spat. 'I collect only originals.'

The monkeys and apes reacted with disbelief and outrage.

'I can assure you it is quite true,' cried a stern voice from the back of the hall, as Robin Pedalbin entered the room. 'And it's quite brilliant! The greatest works can remain safely here in Mrs Van Housen's mansion, where the chosen few such as yourselves will be able to see them. Meanwhile, the rabble who visit the public museum will have decent forgeries to look at – and sneeze on, cough at, poke and prod with their grubby paws, claws or whatever.' He smiled. 'Think of Mrs Van Housen as a defender of art.'

Mrs Van Housen accepted this compliment with a nod. The entire room waited while she carefully finished the banana in her hand and then just as carefully dropped the skin on the floor. 'However,' she continued, 'there are more important questions than simply protecting art.'

Pedalbin frowned uncertainly as the tamarin walked to one of the paintings. 'Consider the painting *See No Evil, Hear No Evil, Speak No Evil*,' she said. 'It is one of our greatest treasures, yet something is clearly missing . . . Anybody?' The audience of wealthy monkeys stared blankly. 'It is missing *clothes*, of course! Here the three monkeys sit, without a stitch of clothing. They are naked . . . nude . . . completely, disgustingly starkers. Who wants to go into an art museum and have THAT staring them in the face?' The tamarin shuddered. 'But do not worry, my friends! Tonight we strike a blow for common decency.' She raised her eyes to the back of the room. 'Mr Gilbo! George!'

The chimpanzee and the gorilla entered, carrying several large tins of paint.

Mrs Van Housen waited until the odd duo were in front of *See No Evil*, then said, 'If you'd do the honours, Mr Gilbo?'

The chimp smirked and dipped a paintbrush into one of the tins. There were gasps of shock and outrage as he began to slap paint on to the masterpiece in front of him. It only took a few seconds, and then he stepped back to admire his handiwork. All three monkeys in the painting were now wearing bright green vests and pants.

The art world of Simian City just sat in stunned silence.

'You can't do that!' cried Pedalbin in horror. 'This isn't what we agreed!' He tried to run forward, but a burly baboon held him back.

'Much better!' declared Mrs Van Housen. 'Now anyone can safely view this picture with their nephew or elderly aunt.'

'You're mad!' cried Pedalbin.

'You're right, I *am* mad,' agreed the golden tamarin. 'Mad that for so long we've allowed *filth* to pass itself off as so-called art.'

Several monkeys began to shout and object, but the baboons made sure that no one left their seat.

The golden tamarin started towards the *Mona Fleasa*. 'And now we come to the most famous painting in the world,' she said sweetly. 'Of course, the real question is – what exactly is she smiling at? A rude joke perhaps? Maybe the perfectly natural – and NOT AT ALL FUNNY – sound of someone passing wind after lunch? One thing is clear – she is smiling at something she SHOULDN'T be smiling at.' Mrs Van Housen displayed her own smile, bright and hard as a diamond. 'Mr Gilbo? I believe in this case a nice green balaclava should wipe the smile off her face . . . literally!'

Gilbo dipped his brush into the tin of paint again. He couldn't hide how much he was enjoying this, but then he became aware of a shadow falling over him. It was George. The gorilla had planted himself between the chimpanzee and the masterpiece.

'George likes the Smiley Lady,' said the gorilla slowly. 'George thinks Smiley Lady is pretty *without* mask.'

'You're not paid to think! You do what I tell you!' snarled the chimp, waving the brush like a weapon. 'And right now I'm telling you to *move*!'

George blinked in deep thought – he liked the Smiley Lady in the picture, but on the other hand, he had always done whatever Gilbo said. It was a tough problem, and tough problems made his brain throb. At last he shuffled slowly backwards. Gilbo sneered and stepped up to the world's most famous masterpiece. His brush hovered centimetres from the canvas and then . . .

A short arrow whizzed down and hit the brush, knocking it out of the ape's hand.

Everybody turned to see where the arrow had come from. There, looking down on the hall from a balcony railing, was a large pig. With small wings on his back, a bow in one hand and a big grin on his face, he looked like a magnificent work of art come to life. He was also completely and utterly starkers, apart from a small pair of bright red swimming trunks, which appeared to be two sizes too small.

'Filth!' shrieked Mrs Van Housen at the startling sight of Peter Porker. 'Nudity in the house! Get it out of my sight!'

Several security baboons started for him, but Pete was already lifting his final arrow to the bow. This one had a rope from one of the long window curtains tied around the end.

Pete fired the arrow high at the wooden panelling above the balcony on the other side of the room. Then, discarding the empty quiver, he gripped the end of the rope with both trotters and swung down to the ground floor.

Gilbo was aware only of a huge pink shape hurtling towards him before it knocked him sideways. And then Pete was on the ground and moving fast. He charged straight for the *Mona Fleasa* and plucked it off the wall. George made a grab for him, but Pete ducked under the gorilla's enormous, muscular arms and ran on. Several baboons charged after him.

'This way!' cried a familiar voice. Pete looked up and saw Curly! Alive! The trainee PiP was looking down over the balcony and there was a little spider monkey with him. They were standing right where Pete's arrow had stuck into the wood. Curly reached over the balcony rail and grabbed the rope that still hung from the arrow down to the floor of the hall. 'Use this, Pete!'

Pete grabbed his end of the rope again, and Curly and the little spider monkey hauled him and the painting up out of the baboons' reach. They continued to pull until the PiPs captain reached the balcony.

Pete wanted to say how pleased he was to see Curly alive and not looking at all like a pancake. However, George the gorilla was already hauling himself up to the balcony.

The little spider monkey pulled Pete over to an open window. 'This is the best way out!' he said.

Pete nodded and stepped out of the open window, hopping from the ledge on to one of the mansion's many roofs. Under the light of the full moon, they seemed to go on forever, studded with dozens of towers and chimneys.

He glanced back at the window and saw the gorilla squeezing its bulk through the frame. Pete knew that he would stand no chance against George.

Quickly the captain began to climb up the closest tower. It wasn't easy with the

Mona Fleasa under one arm, and he was panting by the time he made it to the top. He peered down and saw the gorilla was following him up the tower.

'Give George the Smiley Lady!' demanded the huge gorilla. The squeakiness of his voice didn't make it any less threatening.

'No chance, buddy boy,' shouted Pete, but

as he looked around the rooftops for escape routes, he realized there were none. What he really needed was a plan.

But then he saw something in the night-time sky – something wobbling through the air. As it came closer, he saw that it was a flying-machine! Tammy sat at the front, pedalling for all she was worth. Brian had managed to pull himself up, and now he sat behind the mechanic, urging her to go faster. It didn't look as if Tammy appreciated his advice much.

Pete grinned. He had needed a plan . . . and now one was flying towards him!

CHAPTER 11:

The Secret of the Smile

The flying-machine wasn't far from Pete now, but behind him the tiny bowler hat on the huge head of George the gorilla was coming into view over the tower's edge.

'What's THAT?' cried Tammy, swerving the flying-machine away at the last moment.

Pete knew that the gorilla could turn him into a pile of pork chops in seconds. With nowhere else to run, the captain began to shin up the lightning rod at the top of the tower. It swayed alarmingly in the breeze.

'Fly back this way!' Pete shouted to the

other PiPs. 'I'll throw the painting to you!'

The flying-machine began to swing round in a loop as Pete continued to climb. But the thin metal rod was no match for the full weight of a portly pig! With a horrible snapping sound, it broke near the base and fell sideways. Pete lost his grip and found himself tumbling through the air. Any second now he would plummet and crash into the rooftops below . . .

But, instead, something was keeping him up in the air. Pete turned his head and saw that the lightning rod was now jutting out sideways from the top of the tower. Somehow, as he fell, the back of Pete's trunks had got caught on the end of the pole. The only thing stopping him falling was his trusty Speedios.

George the gorilla was reaching out to him from the top of the tower. 'Give Smiley Lady to George,' he demanded. The gorilla's arm was long, but not long enough.

Pete scanned the skies for the flying-machine.

'It's too dangerous for us to come close!' Tammy yelled to him. 'Throw the painting to Brian as we fly by!'

Pete gave a cool nod, although it's hard to look cool when you're suspended by the back of your trunks – especially when the material of those trunks is beginning to stretch out and give way.

'Full moon's out tonight,' said Tammy, as she steered the flying-machine closer.

Pete counted a beat and then hurled the painting towards Brian, spinning it through the air like Animal Paradise's most decorative – and expensive – Frisbee.

Brian was ready to catch it in both hands and pull it in to his chest, just as he had read in the *Manual of Advanced Catching Techniques*. Unfortunately, it had been a while since

Brian had read this . . . and he dropped the painting.

He looked on in horror as it fell through the night sky, but suddenly a squeaky voice cried, 'NO!' And then a huge figure was leaping from the top of the tower. It was George. His powerful gorilla legs sent him far beyond Pete. He soared out and grabbed his beloved Smiley Lady, the *Mona Fleasa*, in mid-air.

As he began to fall, the gorilla twisted

and hurled the painting back up towards the pigs in the flying-machine. This time Brian caught it safely.

But the PiPs could only watch as George's immense body smashed a hole in the roof below and disappeared.

Brian hugged the *Mona Fleasa* tightly to himself and looked down at the hole in the roof. 'It was beauty killed the beast,' he said softly.

'That's very touching and all,' said Tammy, 'but it'd take more than a fall like that to finish *him* off. Look down there – he's moving!'

The scene inside the mansion was total chaos. Many of the guests were trying to escape. Some baboon guards battled to keep them under control, while others chased Curly around the balcony.

Sensing that the evening wasn't going

according to plan, Mrs Van Housen started screaming, 'Don't leave these disgusting paintings like this! IMPROVE them!' By 'improve them' she meant 'slop house-paint over them'. A couple of baboons dived for paintbrushes and pots. Gilbo had grabbed his brush and tin again, too. A grey woolly monkey was trying to wrestle it from his hands, but the chimpanzee was too strong. He shook his attacker off and scanned the room for a painting to 'improve'.

That's when he heard a crash from above, as George came smashing through the roof.

'George thinks everybody better WATCH OUT!' the gorilla cried in mid-air.

If he'd had time, Gilbo would have shouted back, 'Leave the thinking to me!' But he only had time to say 'Lea–' It didn't matter anyway, because George *was* thinking for once, and what he was thinking was this:

George is going to go SPLAT.

This thought was followed by a second:

George wants a soft landing.

With this in mind, the gorilla arched his back and twisted in the air . . . and landed on top of Gilbo.

The gorilla got up and dusted himself off. 'George is sorry,' he said, looking down at Gilbo lying in the pool of paint squished from his squashed pot. The chimp didn't answer; he was busy sleeping off the effects of one too many large gorillas to the head.

Meanwhile, Tammy had guided the flying-machine down through the hole in the roof and was coming in for a landing. She and Brian both hopped off and, instantly assessing the situation, charged at a baboon who was about to hurl a pot of paint right over a priceless painting. When he saw the two pigs bearing down on him, he wisely dropped the pot and scarpered.

With all this going on, nobody noticed that someone else had climbed on to the flying-machine. One of the baboons was pedalling it and Mrs Van Housen was sitting behind him, barking commands.

She pointed a finger upwards and ordered, 'Driver, take us out of here!'

The machine started to climb into the air, but at that moment, high above the hall, the stretchy material of Peter Porker's trunks could no longer hold the weight of a big-boned pig. They ripped apart at the back and Pete began to fall, straight towards the gorilla-shaped hole in the roof.

Hearing the whistle of air on bare pigskin, Mrs Van Housen looked up from the flying-machine and saw her worst nightmare – a fat hog in nothing but tattered red trunks hurtling towards her.

However, the baboon managed to swerve the flying-machine away just in time. Pete whizzed past them. On the ground below, Gilbo was opening his eyes and sitting up in a daze. He was just asking himself what had happened – and what that whistling sound was that was getting rapidly louder – when Pete landed on him.

Pete peered down at the chimpanzee beneath him, covered in green paint and looking a little flat. 'Hello again,' he said, but Gilbo ignored him, seeming to find it more interesting to be unconscious.

Meanwhile, the flying-machine was heading now towards an open window just beyond the balcony that ran around the room. The baboon pedalled harder and the flying-machine picked up speed. Any second now it would disappear through the window into the starry night beyond and Mrs Van Housen would make her escape.

The tamarin monkey looked back down at the hall and shook a well-manicured fist. 'Stay and wallow in your filth, fools!' she shouted.

Then the flying-machine hit the window with a THUD! – strangely like the THUD of something hitting a solid brick wall.

The machine crumpled and fell to the floor. The window looked completely undamaged. Pete was confused until Curly's face appeared over the balcony railing.

'I asked Vincent to do a quick picture of

an open window on the wall!' he beamed.
'It's pretty good, isn't it?'

It wasn't long before they heard howler
sirens outside and a squad of police
mandrills arrived. A shaken Mrs Van Housen
– her hairdo now bent at an odd angle
– and most of her
baboons were placed
under arrest. The
various monkeys
and pigs were
going around the
room assessing the
damage to the
paintings. Only *See
No Evil* had been directly painted on, but all
of the others had been spattered with paint
in the chaos.

'At least the *Mona* is unharmed,' said
Brian. He looked around. 'Hold on. Where

IS the *Mona Fleasa*? I left it right here!'

Then he spotted Robin Pedalbin scurrying across the crowded room, the famous painting under his furry arm.

'Stop him!' shouted Brian, but in all the noise and confusion, no one seemed to notice.

Pedalbin speed-walked towards the exit. Unfortunately he didn't see the banana skin that Mrs Van Housen had dropped so elegantly on the floor earlier. He skidded forward, his arms windmilling out of control.

Right in front of him, two monkeys were carrying a large painting called *Hippo Reclining on Couch*.

Pedalbin struck the canvas from behind, hitting it head-first and at high speed. There was a terrible ripping sound. His head now poked through, right in the spot where the hippo's head should be. He looked up angrily, as Tammy, Pete and Curly

surrounded him.

Tammy
gazed at him
thoughtfully. 'You
look different,'
she said, 'but
I can't work
out what it is.
Have you done
something new
with your hair,
Mr Pedalbin?'

'The correct way to say my name is . . .
oh, *forget it*!' spat the colobus monkey.

George the gorilla was there to pick up
his beloved Smiley Lady from the floor. He
cradled the painting in his massive arms.
Hurrying across the room to join them all,
Brian looked around at the smiling faces of
the rest of the PiPs. Those smiles looked *very*
familiar.

'That's it!' he cried suddenly. 'The smile on the *Mona Fleasa*'s face! It's the *exact* smile of someone who's just seen a monkey slip on a banana skin and stick his head through a painting!'

The pigs all looked at the grins on each other's faces. They had to agree, they did look a lot like the *Mona*'s smile.

'Brian, I think you've cracked the biggest mystery in the entire art world!' said Pete. With one trotter he held Gilbo's bowler hat over his exposed botty; with the other he gave the medic a high five. It was just bad luck that, once again, there was a bit of paint left on both pigs' trotters; it was even worse luck that, once again, a small splodge flew off, and landed on the *Mona Fleasa* – SPLAT!

At least she didn't have a purple moustache – this time her moustache was bright green.

The pigs looked at each other. 'Oops . . .'

George the gorilla glared at the picture in his hands. He glowered at the pigs who had just ruined it. Then he clenched one massive fist. The two pigs gulped.

But then suddenly Curly threw himself in front of George. 'It's OK!' he cried. 'That isn't the real *Mona Fleasa* either!'

Brian peeked out from behind his trotters. 'What are you talking about?'

Curly turned to the little spider monkey, who was lurking uneasily behind a marble column. 'Tell them, Vincent.'

The little forger giggled nervously. 'I couldn't let her ruin all those lovely old masterpieces. So I did TWO copies of each painting – one to go back to the gallery, and one to give to Mrs Van Housen.'

'Which she *thought* was the original?' said Tammy. 'Brilliant!'

'So where are the real originals?' asked Brian.

Vincent hid his smile behind slender fingers. 'Locked in the basement.'

'Let's go!' said Brian eagerly.

'Wait, Bri!' Pete said. 'There are some nasty security traps down there! I'd better come too.'

With that he popped the bowler hat on his head, turned and headed for the door.

EPILOGUE:

The PiPs learned later that Mrs Van Housen, Pedalbin and Gilbo had all been sentenced to do community service on Monkey Island. They had to paint over graffiti on the buildings of Simian City.

Meanwhile, Vincent had started doing paintings of his own instead of copies of famous works. His first picture was called *Starry Night, with Pig and Gorilla*. Apparently, Speedio Trunks were interested in buying it for their next advertising campaign.

But the real surprise had been George the gorilla. He turned out to be the most talented artist of all. His preferred technique was finger-painting, and he used it to capture his subjects in just a few bold strokes. Many of his pictures were of a smiling monkey. George was going to have his first exhibition at the National Primate Gallery in a month's time.

After the mission, all of the PiPs became more interested in art. Peregrine decided he wanted Brian to paint a portrait of him. With this in mind, he put on his full dress uniform, including all the medals he had been awarded over the years, as well as a couple he'd got in Christmas crackers. He had waxed his moustache so that it stood to attention.

'Make sure you catch my good side,' he told the medic, striking a pose.

'Erm, which is your good side?' asked Brian.

'From the back,' said Lola, walking into

the common room. She had a sequinned dress, massive hair and a big, golden microphone. 'Anyway, Brian said he'd do a painting of *me* today. That's why I've got my pop-star gear on!'

'Oh,' said a disappointed voice from the door. It was Curly with a matching woolly hat, scarf, jumper *and* trousers on. 'I thought you were going to do a painting of me to send to my Nan?'

Tammy pushed her way past the trainee, carrying a stack of pizza boxes. 'That's not what he told me. He said he was going to paint a still-life of pizzas for me. Right, Bri?'

'Er,' said Brian, looking anxiously for a way out.

Then Pete strode into the room. He was dressed in a fetching bathrobe.

'I've been thinking,' said the PiPs captain. 'I can't keep a body like mine under wraps. I'm going to be an artist's model, and you

can be the first to paint me, Brian!' With
these words, he threw back the bathrobe and
let it drop to the floor, revealing a brand-
new pair of electric-blue Speedio trunks,
surrounded by plenty of pink pig. 'Consider
it my gift to the world.'

'Not so fast, Captain! I'm the
commanding officer in this outfit,' spluttered
Peregrine. 'He's going to paint me first!'

'No, me!' cried Lola.

'Me!'

'My pizzas!'

'My gut!'

Brian looked on them in despair. How
was he going to get out of this without
hurting someone's feelings? Then he spotted
something on the floor, just behind the
squabbling pigs. It was the skin from the
banana Tammy had scoffed before the
mission.

Brian smiled to himself. 'I'll do a painting

with *all* of you in it,' he said. 'First, you all
need to take two steps back ...'

All the PiPs took two steps back, and it
was Peregrine who trod on the banana skin.

'ARGHHHHHHH!' he cried out,
grabbing Pete on his way down.

'ARGHHHHHHH!' cried Pete, grabbing
Tammy and Lola.

'ARGHHHHHHH!' cried the girls,
reaching out for Curly as they hit the deck.
All the PiPs collapsed in a gigantic piggy
heap.

'Perfect,' Brian smiled. 'Now just hold
that pose ...'

Crossword

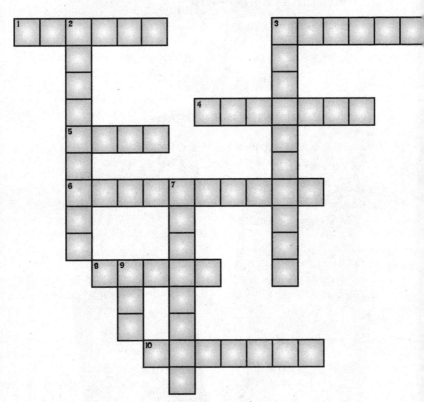

Across →

1. —————— City – the capital of Monkey Island.
3. Pete's code name.
4. Pig Island's famous artist.
5. Curly the statue wears one of these.
6. Gilbo is this type of apew.
8. He's a PiP with arty ambitions.
10. Monkey Island's master forger.

Down ↓

2. The PiPs give the Mona Fleasa a purple one.
7. Robin Le _____ – the National Primate Gallery's chief curator.
9. The colour of Pete's Speedios.

★ Turn to page 150 for the answers.

Wordsearch

Find the words opposite hidden in this grid.
(Look carefully – some may be
backwards or diagonal!)

N	Y	J	K	H	O	I	D	E	E	P	S
T	C	Y	O	G	O	R	I	L	L	A	M
K	E	T	J	P	K	Y	P	W	I	E	U
G	I	L	Q	Y	T	C	L	P	L	E	S
A	M	V	G	H	N	Y	F	L	P	U	E
K	P	N	K	O	K	D	E	U	O	T	U
D	L	H	K	Z	H	B	H	M	M	A	M
A	A	U	N	C	A	C	A	X	B	T	L
Z	S	Y	S	R	P	N	M	J	J	S	Y
Z	T	D	A	H	A	E	G	R	O	E	G
I	E	T	C	N	I	X	V	L	Z	A	L
P	R	X	Q	B	Z	V	P	G	L	H	L

★ Turn to page 150 for the answers.

ARABELLE   PLASTER

NANA   McHOGLET

GEORGE   SPEEDIO

PIZZA   MUSEUM

GORILLA   STATUE

Answers

Crossword

```
 S I M I A N        M R P I N K
   O              O
   U        P I G A S S O
 T O G A        N
   T          F
 C H I M P A N Z E E
   H     E      A
       R E D    S
     B R I A N  A
       E L
       D B
 V I N C E N T
       N
```

Wordsearch

```
N Y J K H O I D E E P S
T C Y O G O R I L L A M
K E T J P K Y P W I E U
G I L Q Y T C L P L E S
A M V G H N Y F L P U E
K P N K O K D E U O T U
D L H K Z H B H M M A M
A A U N C A C A X B T I
Z S Y S R P N M J J S Y
Z T D A H A E G R O E O
I E T C N I X V L Z A I
P R X Q B Z V P G L H I
```